Transitions:
A Middle School Journey

❧

Yimel Hernández-González

Inspiring Lemons Editorial & Publishing

Transitions:
A Middle School Journey

Acknowledgments

I would like to give thanks to God for giving me life. To my Mother who has always been there for me through the bad and good times; to my Dad who encouraged me to write a book. To my family who might be far away to what I now call home but will always be in my heart. Also to my friends and teachers who always listen to my stories and love me. This book is not just for my family and friends, this book is for the hearts I've broken and mended, for the people who lifted me up and broke me down. This book is not just my story, it's a story that every teenager can relate to, it's our story as a society.

Contents

Contents - vii

1

∾

Love

Puppy Love

My love,
your smile is like the sunrise on the morning
of spring days.
Your eyes are the ocean waves
in the Caribbean nights,
which you can never forget or unsee.
Your hands
are like warm fuzzy blankets.
Your skin,
is as white as a pearl,
the kind of pearl that you keep hidden away
in your favorite jewelry box
for fear of it getting lost or hurt

I want to protect you
from the cuts and burns of the world
because your name is what's written and scarred
in my broken heart.

The love that my body contains for you
is slowly feeding upon my tears.

Our Bubble

I feel free, but also trapped.
I have let go of your heart and returned it.
So why is my heart still attached to the blue-eyed boy?

I broke yours into a million pieces,
but I sent mine into the dark desert,
all alone for the aching and thirst for love.

I ripped my heart away from the blue-eyed boy,
so why am I still lost in my own eyes?
It's a maze with no escape or beginning!

A Girl Like Me

She looks into his blue eyes and falls.
I did too and stood back up.
She loves him; he loves her not.
She needs to rise and forgive to forget.
She hates to be able to love or be loved.
She follows her hate and love, as it slowly destroys her.

She forces the love, which is not for her taking,
so she goes to the hate for comfort,
but finds no one there.

The Kiss

He loved her, but she didn't know.
She chose the boy who was right for her.
He kissed her blossom lips, so soft but gentle that he died.
She left her Crystal Knight for Mr. Right.
Little did she know he would be the death of her!

Unrequited Love

He taught me love, while I loved him.
He showed me hate when I had none to give!
He was brighter than the sun, but darker than the night.
He gave me hope, where there was none.

I loved once and again and again.
But, never forget the one that escaped!

The Guard

He is my light at the end of the tunnel.
The keeper of my heart.
The guard of my soul.

The one that makes my spine shiver
my knees weak,
with just the sight of his eyes.

He breaks down all my walls
with just the touch of his lips
so sweet they become poison.
A drug that all of me longs to have.

Having A Heart

Love holds us **down**,
makes us weak,
but it is our strength.

Loving or being loved is living.
Loving someone who lets go **breaks us,**
but builds us up - pain makes us grow.

Foolishness is what killed the cat.
Don't be a cat - be a mighty dog
that howls danger and fright from your heart!

My Heart

I set my heart in a box for no one to hold
but somehow,
you're across the room
piercing into my soul
hypnotizing me,
and I give you the key
to my broken heart,
which you once again hold.

I hand you the key to my heart
within the box for fixing.
But there is no fixing an unlovable soul.
There is only petty.

A Puzzle

He's watching, but not talking.
He is caring, but not loving.

I turn right, he's there,
turn left and he's dead.
Look up, he's gone,
look down, I'm lost.
He left, I fell.
I left; he stands.

The Boy

He chose me, I ignored.
He cared I didn't know.
He loved, and so did I.

His small brown eyes,
and skin as bright as the sun
took me where I couldn't run.

I trapped him, but he owned me.
I cried until I died.

Even in death they stand
not apart or together,
instead, they are one with each other.

Dear Humans

He was foolish, yet kind.
He was intimidating, yet funny;
He was sad but smiled.
She never lost hope but did doubt.

Everyone was and are the same,
yet still completely different.
I wonder why we show our lust and hate,
rather than love and empathy, from our hearts?

We are all wise,
yet we doubt,
and wonder who we really are?

Are we, you, and I the darkness above a mountain?
Or the light hidden beneath a muddy rock?
Who knows?
And who will find the truth?

Am I Broken?

I didn't follow you;
you gave me your sight and I neglected it.
When I tried to steal it back,
I was too late.
I had given you the rest of my hope,
and the key to my heart.
Can I not get it back?

I want to cry
to scream
to hurt you
to hold you
to run with you
but I can't.

I can only stay frozen for they want me to smile,
to be perfect!
They tell me to let go
to forget you,
but how can I forget the gentleness
of your honey silk skin.
The butterflies inside of me,
from your eyes.

Soul's Intertwined

Why is it that every bone in my body
melts by your smile?
Why do I have a million sparks of lightning
shooting out of my lips?
Why does your flawless skin
murder my laugh from satisfaction?
Why is your heart so forbidden from my own?

I see you from 100 miles away
never so close as to feel the touch
of your cold breath
dance along my bare skin,
so rapidly that it was as if there had only been
one breath
one heartbeat
one step.
Until our hearts felt so wicked,
so bad,
yet so right to feel the taste of the forbidden.

Dominator

His evil, yet pure.
He is kind, but hides.

His secrets are told,
but do not unfold.

His scent intoxicates me,
but his smile murders me.

He controls me, yet uses me.
I care, he lies.

Mr. Braces

I've never seen you so clear until now.
Your heart is filled with the same lust
I carry deep beneath my wooden heart.
I can't seem to stop from reveling in the joy
of your embrace.

You moved into a new body
without taking your heart.
Now I wonder, will you ever love?
Or will you join me in hell
to play mind games
and commit sins towards the innocent?

Are you innocent?
Or are you like me?

Desire

My need for you is as strong as a bullet.
I feel the adrenaline
then I feel the pain.
I stop because your smile makes me blush
but your lips make me hush.

I imagine what we could be
but a goal is just a wish without a plan.
So let's make one together
with the love we have for one another.

The Source

This relationship may be intoxicating
but it's feeding my hunger for love each day.

I feel my heart pound and jump
out of my chest from your touch.
I see your lips move as steady as the ocean
I want them to be mine as I am yours.

I crave for your touch and your love
every second of every day!

Resurrection

You have brought me back to life
as I awoke from a dark sleep in hell.
I saw your eyes face mine
so beautiful
I might have been in heaven.

I was a corpse
but then you gave me the kiss of life.
I was lost
and you brought the map.

My Whole

You are my world
my love
my heart
my eyes
my doctor
and the prescription was to love you.
I did as I was told,
now I'm attached.

I am the moon and the stars;
you are my sun and my skies.

You didn't put together the broken pieces
of my heart
instead, you gave me more pieces
for my heart to love and cherish.

The Bus

I see all these rows of people,
but all I can think about is you,
and how alone I feel.

The bright sun shines down on my eyes
and I can finally see the evil in our world.
I wonder if you can protect me from it.
Or am I just falling into an abyss of nothing?

Will I disappear if I breathe?

The Fire In Your Eyes

I saw fire when I looked into your eyes,
and I couldn't look away.
I wasn't scared of you,
I feared us.

I felt myself fading away with you
all of me combined,
like a sculpture melting,
yet frozen.
Your gaze killed me because,
I knew what you were thinking
and what you felt.

I saw your heart break in front of me
and I couldn't look away
I didn't know why you are who you are.
For once I was clueless and lost
all because of you,
A lost boy.

Overthinking

You ignore me
like I'm not here
and the fury of my heart starts to form.
I ask, but you turn away.
I love but you spit at all my deeds.
I decide to hate you but you don't seem to care.

Where do I go?
Who do I choose?
Should I stay?
What should I say?
Should I leave?

Do I stay trapped in a prison full of lies?
Or leave you
and be free
but just as filled with hate and desire.

Two Faced Demon-Lover

I thought you truly loved me.
I believed all your words,
were they just more lies?

I want you to be real
I don't want it to be a dream.
How do I know what is real?
Did you just want our skin to touch
and our lips to meet?
Is your love even real?
Is my love a desire or a dream?

Printed On Me

Your name was always scarred in my heart.
It was like a bullet; the scar always remains.

I erased you,
a stain waiting to be washed away.

Your lips were full of my desires,
now they are just a lost dead thought
roaming through my mind.

Junior

You think I don't know you.
You think I don't love the way you laugh and cry!
You don't believe in my heart or in my mind!
You run away
but the demons will always catch up to you.

You think I will not love you for you,
you're wrong!
I love you
with every breath and fiber in my body.

I want you with all the fire burning in my flesh.
I need you to live,
so believe and rise!

Are We Over?

I can't imagine my life without you.
What will it be with you in it?
I thought I needed you to breathe,
maybe I don't?

When your eyes face mine
my knees go weak
by your crave
by your power!

Were you meant to be mine to hold?

Spring Fire

I ache for your heart,
but I will shed no more tears.

It was like fire falling from my eyes,
freezing on my bare skin.
I felt powerless!

Looking at you is like resigning from life itself.
I can't bear losing you
nor loving you any longer!

Your Heart Is Open

Your skin brushed against mine
and my eyes began to wander over your body.
My heart fluttered
because I've never wanted you this much.
This desire it's almost an obsession,
but I wouldn't trade this feeling for the world.

Your My Past, His My Present

I tasted a bit of what it meant to really be bad
and I loved it!
Was it too much for me to handle?
I wanted you because I knew you wanted me just as much,
but was it ever pure?
Was it ever real?

Did our kiss lay a path to my future?
One neither of you are in.
Should I have kept my lips to myself?

Was the big bad wolf ever bad?
Was I red riding hood,
the innocent one?
Or were you my destiny,
black knight?

Her Family

I've known you for so little
yet your smell intoxicates me,
your lips capture me,
now I can't stop wondering
who is this boy
that affects me so much.

Will I ever be able to get lost
or feel loved from your black brown eyes?
Is everything I've ever felt all a lie,
a mind game I created
but am being played by.

Are you like others?

11

∽

Family

Mother Dearest

Every time you smile at me
I can feel the immense love you have for me
passing through my veins.

Tu eres mi mamá
but the most important thing you are
is my best friend and companion!

My Bridge

Everywhere I go your eyes follow
everything I say you change
anything I feel you hate
the way I walk
talk
sing
breathe.
The way my eyes wander
to places my heart desires,
the way my feet tumble
on the carpet floor
before I may speak my thoughts.
You despise it all .

When I talk there's an excuse,
when I write I'm dull.

I tumble on your bridge,
you laugh and build another one!

The Judger

I see him across the room
smirking
laughing
waiting until the moment
when he can pounce
to eat me alive!

I fear for my safety and joy.
You suck the life out of me
 like a snake devouring a mouse.
You're the snake,
and I have become the mouse!

You took my family as your slaves
and mutated them into hideous demons
who haunt me in my sleep.

DNA

My ancestors history
It's all in me!
I suffocate from their past and their pain.

I feel the course of their disease in my veins
rising to my brain
until my body becomes an iceberg.

In my grave
I dream of being able to feel my heartbeat,
to be able to touch my lips
and let out a single breath of the living
but it is not possible
for my family's ghost follow me
day and night,
from the moment
the sun touched my bare skin
my life was no more,
for they have stolen my purity and fate.
For I have none to spare!

Your Choice

She always chooses him
no matter where I go
what I feel
she chooses him.
I get my hopes up
but she destroys them
and runs to him!

She chooses a stranger
only bonded
and blinded
by an illusion,
rather than her own flesh and blood.
I will not make the same mistake.
But will she decide seeing me being tortured
is better the second time?

Rapunzel

Our friendship is forbidden,
just like love and happiness are for me.
I am the Muppet,
and the witch beyond the black mountain
controls my strings.
Although I wish we could be the picture-perfect friends
we can't.
My heart and my handler
forbade me happiness.

I search for someone to love
my damaged heart
but once they open it
they quiver in fear
of the unknown.
Without knowing that heart belonged to me.
I broke it
before anyone could reach it,
that was the end for me.
I hope you can rebuild the broken pieces
before we both die from the darkness.

My Angel

The world is filled with hatred
and deep desire for the wicked.

At the center of the Earth
there is a light shining so bright
It will make you see the truth
hidden behind the walls of the city.
It is you
my mother
my safe
my guide in the dark forest
my one true friend.
The one who is in it through
thick and thin.
The one who faces the devil himself and laughs
because she knows that all the love in her heart
Is stronger than his will and pull of darkness.

My Tears

I shed my tears for you yesterday
so today I do not cry for you,
I cry for the family I have lost
the one you took from me!

Tomorrow I will cry for the one person
who knew everything about me and stayed!
Tomorrow I will cry for my true love.
But, right now I shall not cry
I will suck the tears dry from my sad eyes
to make sure not one drop falls to the surface!
I will not give you the satisfaction of seeing
my guilt, pain, loss, anger,and regret
from my heart and eyes.

I will start to numb my emotions
just like the generation before me.
I will kill any sense of feelings I have left and at some point
there will be nothing left,
just a girl without a soul.
That is what you have turned me into!

Disappointment

I felt paralyzed;
my knees shattered with hate.
All I wanted,
needed was your love!

I thought you would understand me,
I thought you would know
what feeling alone was like!
Feeling like a failure,
feeling like you're a broken toy
no one can fix.

You used me
lied to me,
all I wanted was you!

The Beauty Of Pet's

I see her,
as she waits in, and day out
for my caress.

She looks out the window,
longing to know
what it would be like to taste fresh air,
to run away,
to be me!
While I wish to be her.

Her burden is being trapped in a jail
which she calls so sweetly hers.
Mine is being trapped in an endless loop
of misery
to what I call life.

My Sidekick

You are my companion,
my best friend,
even my pillow occasionally.

I yearn for your
eyes and your bark
whenever the roses blacken.

A Baby

What is the light of life?

Breathing for the first time,
crying for the first time,
loving for the first time!

A light
so innocent
bright,
and pure
it will relieve you of all your struggles.

Goodbye

What is seeing someone for the last time?
Crying for them for the first time?

Saying goodbye
when you see them in heaven or hell.

Are these feelings of loss ever real?
Or do we make them up
to hide our other wounds!

III

∽

Heaven & Hell

LIFE

A name I know so well as my own,
DEATH!
It calls for me
through the owls pecking down my window.
I hear it from the insects
feeding on my bones
in and out.

A name so sweet follows me
until the day I find my way to hell.
Where the devil himself
is waiting for my presence,
for his wolves to devour my soul
slowly and painfully,
into their wicked bones!

My Body, My Soul

The person in the mirror is a stranger.
She has marks
scars,
bruises
tears
and anger.

It terrifies me
the way the demons have devoured her.
I fight them,
then, they send me
to another century in Hell.
Before I may place a finger on them
or let a single breath
escape from my lips
onto their crocodile skin,
they already have a knife
plunged into my heart.

I cannot E-S-C-A-P-E,
from my body or soul,
I can only suffer!

Middle School

The walls look broken
the ceilings are cracked
the doors are sad and
our hearts are black.

There is some joy,
there's some light.
We're hidden in the dark,
behind our lust and fright.

We try to escape but
these foes are our home
where we have lived and died
together as one,
but alone as no one.

God

The sun's light is ticking
the moon's spark is ending.

For God shall show his mighty wrath
to those who neglect
his way of life.

My life has come to an end,
the closing pages of the chapter
in my book are reaching their end,
is Earth coming with me?

My Faith

Sometimes I do not believe
in what I don't see,
I believe in you
I believe you are my God,
the only God.

That you fly like an eagle high in the sky
watching us all.
I believe you gave up your only son for me.
I believe I am free because of you.

The word hope,
love
kindness
faith
you created for me and my neighbor.

I may feel pain,
but you gave me this pain
to show me I am alive,
that I am free.
It may sound naïve
but that's what faith is isn't it?
To trust no questions asked

Thunder

The pouring rain
splashes onto the ground
with a pounding sense of rage
so quick,
the floor dissolves
the tears of God
who reigns down on the wicked.

A lightning bolt
strikes down from the heavens,
judging all those
impure of heart.

IV

My Story

Anger + Me = HATE

Anger is a part of me
it follows me like a shadow wherever I go.
You're there waiting,
watching
until the moment comes
when we can be united,
to form one with each other.

A monster of hate and fury forms,
the worst part of it all is,
loving the feeling and thoughts of my wicked sins.

Our hate is passing down my spine,
I'm unable to move from all my evil deeds.
Until, I feel myself waking up from a dream
touching my chest
while my heart continues to pump
and burst out of my body
for the thirst of love and happiness.

Fear

The terrifying flickering lights
on their faces scare me away.
The fear of being trapped
in a different world
is a mystery to all men,
but myself.

I scream to the tip of my lungs for help
but no one dares to climb into the brain
of Satan's personal beast
for anyone who touches my heart,
will fall into an eternal pit of fire
straight to Hell!

More Than

I write more than I read.
I talk more than I write.
I feel more than I say,
but I cry more than I should
so my heart falls down a hoop
into a dark root of flame!

My Passion

The sweet melody
of the piano keys
bumping into each other
makes my soul dance
and my body sings.

The rhythm makes my feet skip a beat
which makes me create my own dance.

I've never felt so alive
to breathe in the rhythm of life.

Help Us!

I cry
I scream
I plead for help
but no one cares.
They don't look or listen.

I bleed from my eyes;
they bleed from their laughter.

Is it worth it?
I went through the fury of Hell,
What more can I suffer?
They stole and broke my heart,
but I sold my soul.

Her Sight

Her eyes are so dark,
almost black
so why shall I not yet uncover
the sweet taste of freedom.
I swear and wish to be free from her,
from me, from him, from us.
But I'm still here trapped beneath her eyes.
Or mine?
They are not his eyes or ours
they are mine, yet she has the wheel,
The map,
The control!

Shall I be trapped by their sorrow, or hers.
Not mine or his,
he owns my body,
I own my soul.
While she has my eyes.
Yet I'm here, not blind,
but without color.
She hates it,
while I lost the power to love!

Pain

I fell
couldn't get up,
couldn't move.
My legs were paralyzed
but my heart was beating
through the pain!
I climbed so high;
I couldn't cry.
I fell so fast I couldn't die.

Your pain is mine,
but with their pain I die.
Pain killed me but taught me!
I loved and hated it.

Numb

Even though I'm surrounded by people,
I'm all alone in this world.
I laugh
I scream
I have sad
and happy moments
but no family and no friends.

It makes me numb
thinking that I could love again,
those who "love me,"
hate and hurt me
without the blink of an eye.

My Attack

The pain might hurt me,
but my heart is what kills me!

My disease is eating me alive
but I can't help enjoying
the suffocating and peeling of my skin.

If I die,
I know my enemies will rot beneath me
during my stay in Hell
If they don't,
I will climb back
into the living world to see them,
to make them eat and drink
their rotting flesh,
to rip their bones apart,
to feel the pain
I felt and enjoyed it!

My Ears

Have you ever felt like you were drowning alive?
You say or feel something
but everyone else
prohibits you from doing so?

Feeling powerless for a person like me
Is dying without ever living!
What everyone else does
is just pull the trigger.

I hear my name in your throat and
all I feel is you pulling my heart
out of my chest.

Springs Coming

People ask
Why does it rain?
Why do the skies cry
beneath our eyes?
We stay silent
not knowing
or wanting
to see the world in front of us.

We walk
we fall
we run and
we break.
What's the point of it all?

Why do the branches break with our breath?
Why do the leaf's die with our hearts?
Why are we slaves to our body,
heart and mind?

Be Yourself

We wonder who we are?
What our purpose is.
I'll tell you what it is
embrace the light
in your flesh and blood
show your colors and wonders
your spirit and might
your hope and your courage
show the world who you really are,
before they find out!

Surroundings

You shun me before I can speak,
so I hush you in your sleep.

You look at me with demise
so he killed you with despise.

What love is your hate?
What hate is your love?

You shall burn with the stake!

Summer Is Coming

The sky's awake
the flowers begin to bloom
and my heart begins to rise!

I've never felt so alive,
yet so dull.
The wind howls in the night
and I wish to be free of this prison.

The bees buzz,
but I'm still numb,
still paralyzed,
still dying.

This pain was caused by all the vile,
but my revenge will come!

Our Colors

Grass is green
bricks are red,
Your heart is gold
and mine is black.

Love is blind
the sky is high
but that didn't stop us
from changing our eyes.

Rotting Inside

I feel the blazing fury of my anger
running through my veins.

All I sense is my heart in my throat
ready to burst out of my chest.

Do you ever want to scream
until your lungs run out of air?
Well, I do!!
You never really know why
until you cry alone.

Women

I remember when the boys who became men
ripped your clothes
as easily as they killed pigs.

I remember you women calling your husband
while they took your pride and dignity away
but pride and dignity
can neither be taken nor given.

I summon you women
know now that I call you
warriors and survivors.
Not slaves, not fools.
What women is a fool for falling in love
with a man whose only love
is the flesh on our bones.

I kneel on this day
and am proud to call you a soldier
For surviving the battlefield
which is a man.

Queens

We who keep the world
balanced are struck down.

Women,
who are like leaves
that blow in the wind
so delicate
so gentle
are struck down in their pride
by men who believe they rule us.

We are the real warriors,
The ones who wear our hearts
on our sleeves.

Mistake

I feel
shamed
disgraced
opened to this new world
I didn't know existed.

I wanted to ←←reverse the past
but what was done was done
I set my future to a wicked path
It was my undoing.

I hurt you,
but it also hurt me
I would come out of this changed
from life itself.

I Am

I am bright and uptight!
I wonder what I will become?
I hear myself cry, I hear myself laugh, I hear myself lie...
I see love and hate.
I want to be free to be able to move on.

I am bright and uptight!
I pretend to be tough, but I feel broken inside.
I touch my bare skin to wash away my tears.
I worry the demons will see the real me.
I cry for my heart and bones.

I am bright and uptight!
I understand that I may smile, all the time, but the pain is with me, all the time.
I say that I believe that someday the demons will smile for me, not at me.
I dream of moons and stars shining for my path to follow.
I try to work things out even though they might not work.
I hope for forgiveness, compassion and most of all respect!

I am bright and uptight!

V

Enemies

Cowards

I see you across the hall
laughing
staring
pointing.

I know you better than you think I do,
but ◊you◊, well let's say,
you don't know the first thing about ◊me◊

You think I'm dumb,
well I'm not!
Your little games won't work on me
anymore.

I see behind those masks you have on,
if you don't take them off, you'll regret it!!
On the day the sun finally reaches your eyes,
those masks you have
will finally fall to the darkest place on Earth.
but if you don't open your eyes soon
it might be too late.

Deception

Today you're my friend,
tomorrow you're not.
Your two-faced,
so am I,
you fooled me,
I can do the same.

I see you lying to yourself,
your own heart and soul,
the sad thing is,
you believe your lies.

Today, you love me.
Yesterday you destroyed me.
You're no saint, but am I?

Their Kindness

I pray for their love,
as I gave them mine.
They rather spit at my good deeds
then revel in the joy of love.

I forgive,
forget,
turn the other cheek.
Yet all they do is spread
wicked sins towards my soul.

They scratch my heart with a blade
which will never be cured.
I try and try to mend the damage of my heart.
but nothing will work,
because they might be evil,
but I'm wicked!

Voices

I cannot speak,
I cannot laugh or smile.

I am trapped in my own misery,
in a prison,
a box of my own making.

They tell me to look away
to protect the secrets
they keep deep within their wicked hearts.

How can I keep a secret
when there is a plan to kill me?
How can I stay quiet while I suffer?

About the Book

Transitions is my own written collection of poems I wrote throughout middle school. It's about romance, one's first love, and their most epic. Hell and heaven, what awaits there, and the demons out in this world. Families ups and downs and the pressure that comes with being part of any family. Our enemies out in this world, people who might have been friends or a loved one, and how their betrayal or allegiance affects us. I wrote what I felt and what I knew others might be going through. To show that there is someone out there who cares and understands.

CPSIA information can be obtained
at www.ICGtesting.com
Printed in the USA
LVHW090834180222
711257LV00021BA/902

9 780578 352930